THE ULTIMATE DESIRES

PRABHJOT K SAINI

Become Shakespeare.com

First published in 2018 by

Becomeshakespeare.com

Wordit Content Design & Editing Services Pvt Ltd
Unit - 26, Building A -1, Nr Wadala RTO,
Wadala (East), Mumbai 400037, India
T: +91 8080226699

Copyright © 2018, Prabhjot K Saini

©

ISBN - 978-93-88930-21-5

ABOUT THE AUTHOR

Prabhjot K Saini is an Engineer by profession working in Healthcare Industry in Bangalore, India. She has been working since 2006 in Software Engineering for healthcare products.

Writing is one her strong passions and she has over 250 blogs and fictional stories published online on candlesonline. wordpress.com, Searchwarp.com, yourstoryclub.com and soulofwit.com. Most of the content for her blogs comes from her own experiences of daily life that she sees around herself. Her articles have been published in webzines and magazines including Candles, Femina and Mind Creative.

One of her short stories has also been published in a short story collection named, "Your's Lovingly".

She was also involved in freelance writing where she used to write promotional articles on fabric fashion, jewellery fashion and travel.

She believes in the power of oneself and re-alignment of one's thoughts with the Universe. She is highly spiritual and believes in her own God. She has invested a lot of time in understanding herself for she believes that only by getting the inner peace can one really succeed in life.

She is also a strong feminist and writes extensively against objectification of women's bodies and assumed incapability of women in intellectual and sports arena.

Her husband; Kapil has always encouraged her every endeavour.

CONTENTS

A World of Innocence

'Mummy, where do babies come from?' asked Rishika, holding her Barbie doll in one hand.

She had just returned from the hospital with her mother after visiting Aunt Manju and her new born baby

Before Rishika's mother, Tanuja could think of a reply, another question came shooting at her.

'Mummy Mummy, why was Manju Aunty on the hospital bed?'

Tanuja could not help but smile looking at her five-year-old daughter's eyes twinkling with curiosity, trying to understand the world.

'Do they all come from the hospital? Where do doctors get them from? Which hospital did you get me from, Mummy?'

'Take a breath, Rishika. First, let me look for the keys. I will answer all your questions while driving back home, OK?'

'"OK, replied Rishika, and patiently waited for her mom to hunt for car keys in her bag and unlock the car. She quickly hopped onto the front seat, while her mother put on both the seat belts.

'Now tell me, where do doctors get the babies from?' asked Rishika, not giving up.

'Did you notice how fat Manju Aunty had become before she had the baby?' asked Tanuja.

Rishika nodded listening intently.

'It was because the baby was in Manju Aunty's tummy. So, the doctor got the baby out of her tummy,' elaborated Tanuja.

Rishika kept staring at her mother for a while without blinking.

'But how did the baby get in there?' she asked next.

This time, it was Tanuja's turn to be surprised. She did not expect this question. Thus, she was confused about how to answer this.

However, before she could think of something, Rishika came up with an answer of her own.

'I guess I know how. Manju Aunty might have eaten the seed that can grow babies and the baby grew up in her tummy. Just like we plant seeds in soil, and after a few days they become plants. Am I right, Mummy?' said Rishika, beaming.

Shocked, Tanuja pulled over the car. She was amazed at how far could a five-year-old brain think.

'No, that is not true! Baby was made inside her tummy. A part of Manju Aunty and Ravi Uncle together created the baby which grew for a few months in Manju Aunty's tummy and when the baby was big enough, doctors removed him from the tummy so that the little baby could grow up like you.'

Though Rishika still looked perplexed, she bought the explanation.

'Oh, is that the reason everybody said that baby's nose is like Ravi Uncle?' asked Rishika, trying hard to make sense of the new knowledge.

'Yes, my darling.'

'Was I also made in your tummy? Have I come from there?'

'Yes sweetie.'

'Do I look like Dad because he and you created me together?'

Tanuja did not know what to say. She did not know how Rishika was taking all this. Though she replied in affirmation, she was confused about if she did the right thing by telling her the truth rather than some story about a fairy coming with a baby and giving to the mother. Tanuja never wanted to tell false stories to her daughter. She felt that it was important to tell kids the truth in a form that was not dirty or revealing, but still the truth. She was quite curious to know what her little head would think of next.

Rishika did not come up with any more questions now. They reached their destination and she hopped out of the car to go play with her best friend in the neighbourhood. Tanuja got busy with the household work but she could not stop thinking about Rishika's questions. She realised that the kids see the world in a totally different light, far different from an adult's view of the world.

Rishika was very talkative with limitless capacity of words. Sometimes they meant something, sometimes they did not. Sometimes Tanuja listened to her in awe and at other times, she had to beg Rishika to stop talking.

The other day, Rishika and her friend, Tina, were in the backyard when they decided to make artificial wings so that they could also fly like birds. No matter how much Tanuja tried to explain them they cannot, they simply would not give it up. They used cardboard and thermocol to make wings. Unfortunately, all their efforts were in vain. Tanuja felt sorry looking at their efforts go in vain, but in no time, both the girls were back on another project, which was to make a kennel for the puppies nearby.

A female dog in the neighbourhood had given birth to five pups around a month ago. Rishika was totally enchanted with those small creatures. She wanted to get them home, but of course, Mummy would not allow. Finally, when Tanuja conceded to Rishika's wish and allowed the puppies to stay in the backyard, the girls were absolutely thrilled. In no time, the girls pulled up a carton box to make a small home for the new additions to the family.

Tanuja was very proud of her little girl. Not only was Rishika intelligent and smart but also quite sensitive. When she was even younger, she would feel extremely sorry at the sight of child beggars on the road. And all sorts of questions would come again and again.

'Mummy, who will take care of that child? He is crying and is also very dirty.'

'You have so many coins in your purse. Please give one to that child,' often begged Rishika.

Then one day, Tanuja decided to tell her little girl the reality.

'Rishu, these children do have parents but they don't do any work because they send their children out to beg and get money for them. If we keep giving them money, the parents of these children will never work.'

Rishika was quite startled.

'Why would parents send the children to beg on the streets?' asked Rishika with tears in her eyes.

'Baby, these parents don't have money and they have found an easy way to get money from us. So, they don't have to work themselves. It is our responsibility to not give them money so that the parents of these kids are forced to do some work, earn money and send the children to school where they rightfully belong. Begging is not good, sweetie, and just because we have a lot of coins we should not encourage it either.'

This time, Rishika was confused but she looked convinced. There were no more questions from her side, but she became very gloomy after the discussion. Tanuja hated the fact that in her attempt to introduce her daughter to the real world unintentionally she injected some negativity into her daughter's little heart.

Rishika missed her dad a lot and would not let a day go by without talking to him on Skype. Tanuja's husband, Arun, was away on a business trip to London for a year. Tanuja had decided to stay back for the sake of her own career and also because they did not want to disturb Rishika's schooling. Rishika would talk hours and hours on internet. Even when both mum and dad got tired, she would not stop.

A few days later, both mother and daughter decided to visit one of their relatives, Tanuja's sister-in-law, Reena and her husband, Abhay. They were a nice family and had helped Reena's family a lot during rough times. It was just a general visit with no fixed agenda.

Though Tanuja and Reena were not very emotionally attached, they shared a common interest of cooking. So, every time they met, there was a huge discussion on recipes and cooking experience. Rishika obviously used to get bored after watching so much Cartoon Network and would pester her mum to return to home.

This time, Abhay was home for a change, and as Tanuja knew, he loved kids. Thus, in no time, Rishika was totally enjoying playing games with her Uncle Abhay.

While Tanuja and Reena were busy in the kitchen chatting, they suddenly heard Rishika cry out. Confused and scared, the first thought that came to Tanuja was that her daughter had fallen or hurt herself somehow. As soon as they reached the living room, what they saw shocked them.

While Rishika was sitting on the floor hugging her legs and looking scared, her Uncle Abhay was just getting up from the sofa. He looked tensed.

'Oh! It's nothing. I was just tickling her when she fell on the floor and cried,' Abhay explained, smiling nervously.

As soon as Rishika saw her mother, she ran to her and hugged her tightly.

Tanuja felt that she was trembling.

'What is it, Rishu? What happened?'

'Mummy, Uncle was giving me the *bad touch*. So, I shouted like you had asked me to. We were tickling each other and then he said that he knows an interesting game to play.' Rishika narrated innocently as she looked at Tanuja with moistened eyes.

She was not crying; she was just upset because she felt uncomfortable.

Tanuja looked furiously at Abhay; she had never known she could ever get this angry. Her face blushed with anger and unable to control the tone of her voice, she shouted 'How could you, Abhay? How dare you even think that you could do something like this to my daughter?'

'Your kid is lying. I did not do anything. I was only tickling her. I don't know what kind of education you give your kids. They have no sense of respect for elders. How can a 5 year old girl ever make such an accusation on me? Reena, can you believe this? Do you believe this kid?' shouted Abhay in his defence.

Reena was too shocked to respond, and. Rishika was crying profusely by now. She did not like this fight among the adults. Tanuja picked up all her belongings and rushed out of the house with her daughter. She was still angry and now she couldn't even control her tears.

Reena came behind them, but in no vain, the car had already sped away.

Tanuja knew she had to stop crying and take control of her emotions. She had to understand what really had happened. She composed herself somehow and looked at Rishika, who was continuously staring at her mum.

'Mummy, why are you crying?' asked Rishika, crying herself.

'Baby, your Mummy really loves you. You have to tell me what really happened there. Don't feel shy, just tell me what happened.'

'Uncle was tickling me on my neck and underarms and before that we were pillow fighting. I was really enjoying the game. But then, he stopped tickling and said that he has another interesting game to play. He also said that I should not tell anybody about this game. I agreed. He then took me in his lap and slid his hands inside my frock. I thought he was going to tickle, but he did not. I did not like it. I remembered what you had told me about the bad touch. So, I just shouted and ran away from him. Mummy, I am not lying. I swear on God, it was the bad touch,' said Rishika with tears flowing down her cheeks.

Tanuja hugged her immediately and said, 'I know, baby. I know that you are not lying. You will never lie.'

Both mother and daughter hugged each other for long. Tanuja felt huge emotions. She felt extremely angry and cheated by her own family. She felt very sorry for her daughter but at the same time, she felt proud of her too. Her daughter had finally done something that she could never do as a child. Her daughter had the courage to go out and tell the world that something wrong happened. Her daughter was not a victim, but a winner. She was an inspiration.

'Rishu, listen to me very carefully. You know what, Mummy is very proud of you. You did the right thing by shouting and calling out to me. Nobody has the right to touch you badly. Just remember, if another time such a thing happens, you have to do the same thing that you did today. You have to shout and call out to all the adults around you and tell them what happened without feeling any shame or guilt. It is not your fault, baby. Uncle was wrong, he is bad. You are my baby, very pure and very brave.'

'Mummy, why did Uncle say that I was lying? I am not lying. Why did he say bad things about me to Reena Aunty?'

'Because Uncle knew that he did something wrong. He did something that he shouldn't have done. And you don't have to feel bad about whatever I said to him. He had to be told that it was his fault. You are not wrong, baby. He is.'

Rishika gave her million dollar smile, finally. She was now convinced that her Mummy really meant what she said.

Tanuja knew that this was the first incident in her daughter's life and many more were to come her way. However, she felt extremely proud of herself. She was bringing up a brave and outspoken girl, a girl who would grow up to be a confident woman. She would never doubt herself. She would protest against all wrongs around her. She would not be victimised to take blame or shame on herself. Tanuja was a proud mother today.

Suddenly her train of thought got interrupted by just one thought which lingered in her mind – *only if my Mom had told me about the bad touch, only if she had taught me to be this courageous. Only if I had not taken the blame* and shame on myself, only if I had not suffered so many years for those few evenings, I would have been a very different person.

ABANDONED

One day, a year ago, I woke up feeling different. Everybody in my family looked sad and gloomy. Though they were extremely busy packing things up, some three more people were in the house to help them pack and put things in big boxes which were then placed in a monster truck. The only things that were not being packed were mine. Feeling anxious, I tried to chase the three strangers away, but Mom and Dad stopped me. I then remembered that two years ago also when we vacated our previous home and shifted to this new one, everybody had been packing large boxes in a monster truck. But this time they looked really dejected.

My family includes my parents and my sister, Riya. They adopted me when I was just a month old. I have very indistinct memories of meeting them for the first time. I just remember being terrified. Riya was only six years old then; she used to scream at every sight of me. I was very scared of her too and always felt that she would hit me with one of her toys. Mom and Dad eventually succeeded in making us best of friends.

After spending four years with Riya, we became inseparable. She used to sleep with me, feed me, play with me and even complained to me about Mom and Dad. Every day when she returned from school in the afternoon, I used to be at the gate to welcome her, wagging my tail, jumping up to lick her face. She didn't like me doing that and Mom had strictly told me not to do so. Instead, Riya let me lick her hands and legs. While she used to eat her lunch, she would also feed me bits of her food. She taught me to shake hands with her and even give her a hi-five. She used to toss my bone away for me to go and fetch it for her. I loved to watch her laugh the way she did. In the evening, we chased each other on the terrace. Sometimes she let me play with her friends who had come over. I loved Riya a lot. I still do.

Mom and Dad were very happy to see Riya and me getting along so well. I remember when I was a small baby, I used to poop and pee wherever I felt comfortable. I used to get scolded by Mom every time. It took me some time to understand that Mom was very happy when such things were done outside the gate. She would also give me that yummy chicken chewy and called me 'Good Boy' when I complied with this behaviour. I never liked the feel and smell of her when she was upset. In fact, I even stopped licking anything in the kitchen and biting on any footwear or chewing on newspaper around. I stopped disturbing them while they ate their food. I think, I was an obedient five-year-old smart, white-coloured Labrador. My name is Doodle.

A couple of years ago, Dad forgot to lock the gate at night and even the front door was left open. He must have been very tired that night, otherwise he always locked all the doors before going to bed. I was worried about it. I licked his nose a number of times to wake him up, but he wouldn't wake up. I did not want to bark and wake everybody up, so I just stayed near the gate to make sure nobody entered my home. It was a cold night and I stayed below the car in the porch. In the morning when Mom woke up, she saw the door left ajar. She came to pick up the milk packets and saw me sitting upright at the gate. She patted me a lot that day. I was also given that special mutton and beef. Dad was very happy with me too. I understood then that I had done my duty well and it is my responsibility to protect my house.

There were days when Dad woke up late and I wanted to go for a walk. I would then lick his nose and he would know that I was desperate to go out. Other times, I would just sit at the gate and wag my tail and Dad would then come with my leash and take me for a walk. I loved the smell of fresh world early in the morning or late evening.

Even though, Mom and Dad had busy schedules, they never forgot to feed me and take me out for regular walks every morning and evening, except when they had fights among themselves. Riya and I would usually sit silently in our room when Mom and Dad shouted at each other. Sometimes Riya would start crying; I never understood why. But I didn't like to see her cry, so I would go and start licking her face. Then I would just curl up in her lap and she would hug me for a long time.

Couple of months before the day of packing, the fights had escalated. Mom and Dad argued all the time and Riya used to get very upset. She used to hug me and cry for long periods of time. The night before, she simply would not let go of me and I couldn't know what was wrong with her. Even Mom and Dad were very upset and they kept telling me that they'll miss me a lot. Riya started fighting with them and refused to eat. She kept telling them, 'I cannot live without Doodle.' She wanted to take me along with them. Dad then took her to the other room and shut the door.

I was very sad to see all this. I knew that I had not done anything wrong. I had not licked any of their utensils or torn any of the sandals and I definitely had not done a poo or a pee inside the house. Why were they so upset with me?

Mom then moved my kennel and bed sheets outside the garden gate together with my water bowl filled with clean water and food bowl filled with my favourite chicken liver. And then I knew that they were going away, leaving me behind. By then, the truck with all those boxes had gone and a yellow car stood outside waiting for them.

I couldn't bear it anymore; I couldn't even imagine that they were leaving. I quickly jumped into the back of the yellow car. Dad wasn't angry; he simply took me in his arms and patted me. For the first time, I saw tears in his eyes.

'Sorry Doodle,' he said. 'We cannot take you to Australia. I have asked the dog care to come and get you. I hope you find a better family and loving parents.'

I started licking him, trying to tell him that I really love him and I don't want a better family. I just want them. I wish they could understand how broken I felt. Mom kept on crying. She kissed me and said that they'll miss me a lot. Riya would not let go of me and Dad had to pull her away. They got into the car and it started pulling away slowly. I felt desperate and started chasing the car. I could see Riya's face through the rear window, tears flowing down her cheeks. I ran as fast as I could and my breath quickened. My throat ran dry and I wanted some water. But more than anything else, I wanted my family back. My legs ached but I ran even faster to catch up with them. The car soon vanished at the next set of traffic lights.

I hung around the traffic lights for a long time, but there was no smell or sign of them. I came back home only to find my food and water was gone and my kennel was broken into by other dogs. I was very hungry and thirsty, but I wanted to wait for Riya to come and feed me. I missed my bed and comfort but more than that, I missed those hugs and kisses from Riya.

It has almost been a year now since my family departed. I sleep outside the garden gate and the new occupants of the house feed me at times. My new home is now an abandoned drainage pipe. I don't like to play with stray dogs, I have no friends and my life is very lonely. Nobody has given me a bath since a year. I do get wet in the rain but then I feel very cold. I sometimes sleep under the traffic lights where the yellow car disappeared but still there is no trace of my family. I cannot understand what happened. I never did anything wrong; I never misbehaved and Mom always said that I am a good boy. Why did they abandon me then?

Today I am not feeling well and I have an acute pain in my stomach since morning. I don't feel like eating the food that the new home owners have dropped off. I am still waiting for Riya to feed me. The pain is getting progressively worse and I am curled up in the shade to escape from the harsh heat of the sun. My breath is slowing down and I think that something is killing me. I am feeling a little scared.

I remember a few months before my family left, I had a similar pain and Dad had taken me to the hospital. I hated it but the nice doctor had given me an injection that made me feel better immediately. I had slept very peacefully that night by Riya's side after a dinner of rice and yogurt. I miss Dad today. He could have taken me to the hospital. They might still return and heal me. I do not want to go outside my sordid home; it makes me feel so much better inside.

I cannot keep my eyes open anymore and the pain seems to be getting distant. Riya's face keeps on appearing through the mist of darkness that is spreading in front of my eyes. I am finding it hard to breathe now. After that last long breath... even my pain seems to have disappeared. There is only darkness around... and nothingness. I feel free of all pain and hurt.

At last... after being abandoned... I feel good... I feel liberated.

AND SO IS THE LAW OF NATURE

'Mummy, I think Olive is not well,' Sia came running to her mom.

'Let Olive rest, Sia. You are getting obsessed with her,' Mom snapped back.

Sia was just told by her mom not to disturb her as she was doing some very important work. Mom was busy on her laptop. Sia couldn't take the fact that Olive was still in her nest and was just not ready to come out. She usually came out every morning, flew some long distances, got some more twigs and attached it to her nest. But today, she was still inside her nest.

Olive and Pine were two cute pigeons who had made Sia's balcony their permanent residence. For the last one week, both of them had been building up the nest with small twigs and leaves. Five year-old Sia was amazed at Olive and Pine's creativity to build such a beautiful and strong nest with just a beak; they had no hands after all. She came around her mom to ask a million questions about why pigeons don't stay in strong homes like theirs.

'They will get wet in the rain, Mummy. How will they protect themselves from rain storms?'

'Mummy, what will happen if an earthquake comes? Their nest will get destroyed? Why can't we build a nice big house of bricks and cement for them?'

'Mummy, where did Olive and Pine stay before building this nest? Why did they change their home? Did they not have enough friends in their previous home?'

Sia had innumerable questions about Olive and Pine. She was the one to come up with the names. While they were building the nest, Sia was having her favourite Veggie pasta. She dropped a small piece of the pasta, but Olive did not take it. Then she dropped a piece of onion, Olive was not interested in that either. Finally, she dropped a piece of Olive and pigeon just took it in its nest. That's how she got her name – Olive. And then the name Pine came naturally to her. Dad helped her understand which one was female and which was male. Olive had a little ring around her neck and that's how she is the female. Since the day she noticed these pigeons coming with twigs in her balcony behind her old tri-cycle, she was totally enchanted. It became her habit to check on them almost every hour when she was home. She wouldn't eat her food after coming from school, till she found both of them back in the nest. By now, she knew the entire schedule of the birds and a bit of anomaly to that schedule would make Sia very worried.

Since morning today, Olive did not come out of her nest. Sia was getting worried if Olive was down with flu or cold since it rained a bit last night. Pine was not there, he must have been out since long.

'Mummy, can you check Olive's temperature using my thermometer? She doesn't look too well.' Sia said as she came with some tiny bits of chapatti to feed Olive. But the bird did not move. She saw Pine come in after some time and sit close to Olive. He kept giving her rubs from the beak. When Sia left the chapatti bits on the floor, Pine flew and got the bits for Olive and also ate some of them himself. But Olive was just not moving. It was time for Sia to go to her cousin's place, but she was really worried.

'Why is Mummy not taking Olive to a doctor, Olive is not well and she is not taking it seriously?' Sia thought, upset with her mom, she simply went away to her cousin's place as she knew that disturbing Mummy during office work can get her a good scolding.

Sia came back after three hours and found that now Pine was sitting on the middle of the nest and Olive was doing all the work. She did not understand, earlier it was the other way round.

'Mummy, what are Olive and Pine doing? It looks like they are hiding something.'

Mummy came down to check on the birds and realized Olive had laid an egg and now they are taking turns while sitting on it. Mummy explained to Sia, that Olive and Pine have a little egg, which will give them a baby, so they both are protecting the egg from cold while sitting on it. Sia was shocked initially, then happily surprised and eventually she was super excited. She called up her cousins and her friends to let them know that Olive and Pine have an egg. Now Olive became Mummy Olive, Pine became Dad Pine and the little one became Baby Sia.

Next three weeks were totally enthralling for Sia. She couldn't wait for the egg to hatch. And finally one day the egg hatched and out came the baby Pigeon, Sia named it Basky. It looked like a little pink ball. Olive and Pine took extreme care of Basky; they fed him, protected him and made the nest even stronger, with a lot more twigs. Sia was worried initially if the Basky was born fine or not. Mummy and Dad convinced her that she need not worry, baby Pigeons looked like that.

Mummy Olive wouldn't leave Basky at all. Father Pine would go and get the food and stay near them all the time. They looked like a perfect family to Sia, just like her own – Mummy, Dad and little Sia. They spent time together, they stayed close together, Mummy spent more time with her while working on her laptop, Dad worked out of home and came only in the evenings. Sia saw her own little family in that family of birds.

Slowly and gradually Basky started developing feathers and looked more like a pigeon. He was already three weeks old and Olive and Pine were more confident in leaving him alone. Basky started coming near Sia without fear now. Sia also could see that Basky is perfectly normal bird. Life seems to be taking its own shape.

Just a month old, and she saw Pine teaching little Basky how to flutter its feathers. Basky started to take little flights from one corner of balcony to the other.

'Mummy, Olive and Pine aren't going to send Basky to school to learn how to fly?' Sia asked. And she was told that birds don't have schools, parents teach the babies themselves. She was disappointed. 'How would Basky make friends and play games, if he doesn't go to school?' She thought 'This world needs a school for birds also,' Sia declared one day on the dining table. Mummy and Dad just laughed.

A week later Basky was confident in going around long flights on his own. But Sia was sad now, she saw much less of him. Nest was almost empty now. Olive and Pine would also come once in a while when she would keep food for them. After two days of loneliness, she burst out into tears, Why did Basky leave?' she asked Mummy.

'This is the law of nature. Once babies grow up, they leave parents to take care of their own lives and live independently,' Mummy said.

'What does that mean?' Sia asked still crying terribly.

'That means, Basky is a grown up now and doesn't need Mummy and Dad, he can get his food himself and protect himself. So he has gone,' Mummy explained.

Sia was quite for a while and in a deep thought. She then asked, 'Will I also fly away one day to live away from you? Is that why I am growing up? Is this the reason you are sending me to school so that I learn to fly away from you?' She had a trembling in her voice. She had just discovered a truth about life and she happened to be disappointed by it. She had dreamt of living with her parents, her family forever. She had believed that Olive, Pine and Basky would continue to live with them forever. And she suddenly did not want to grow up because she did not want to fly away.

Mummy couldn't control her tears as well, 'There is a lot of time, Sia. You will fly away but not far from us.'

Mummy and baby Sia hugged each other for long. And two blocks away Olive and Pine were preparing another nest in somebody else's balcony for another baby Sia.

COMPLICATED RELATIONSHIPS

Neeraj had no clue what to do. He was stuck. His conscience didn't allow him to leave Abha and his heart didn't allow her to leave Shiksha. All he felt for Abha was pity, if today she came and told him happily that she had found somebody else who really loved her the way she deserved, it would be the happiest day for him. He simply could not see her cry and he was ready to give her all that she wanted just because she had nobody apart from him. 'What would she do, if he left her alone? Who will take care of her?' he wondered. She would be broken to pieces; she'd probably go into depression and suffer a lot. But she anyways was suffering now also. This was not the kind of marriage she had dreamt of.

'I tried my best to love her, to feel those feelings of love for her, the feelings that I have for Shiksha. But it simply is not possible.'

Shiksha on the other hand was Neeraj's tennis partner. They had met six months ago. Neeraj and Abha got married a year ago and they had known each other since last three years. They were in love with each other, at least that's what Abha believed. After Abha's parents died in a car crash, she was hit by depression. She was very dependent on her dad and simply needed a lot of emotional support. This was when Neeraj, who was her colleague then, started showing interest in her. He supported her in all sort of ways, exactly the way he would do for somebody of his own family. He would make her smile, take her out for movies, gave her a wonderful friend circle, had fun with her, and made her happy in every way. In no time, Abha knew that he was the guy for her. He too felt for her then, he realized that he loved her company. He loved to make her happy, to do all that was possible to get that smiling face.

'What else could I ask for in a girl, she is beautiful and caring? My parents love her. I think she is right one for Me.' thought Neeraj. They loved each other and believed that it was the right thing to get married to each other. Abha, being a very traditional girl, did not want to engage in sexual intimacy till they got married and Neeraj being an understanding partner never tried to persuade her.

They got married and within a month, Neeraj realized that the fire was missing. That spark of love, that touching feel that romantic closeness, that warmth was missing.

It was not her fault; she was the way she was. 'Why does he behave so weird when it comes to sex? He doesn't say anything. I am doing all that I am supposed to do. What am I doing wrong?' thought Abha. She simply did not understand that they could not connect at physical level at all.

Within six months of marriage, Neeraj was frustrated and did not know what to do. Abha was emotionally very dependent. Even when she had a light fever, she needed him around. Some politics in office disturbed her so much, that she needed Neeraj for support. He tried to make her understand that he couldn't be around all the time; she had to handle things on her own. But whenever he tried to talk her out, it would get worse. There was no getting out of it.

And then he met Shiksha in his tennis practice – beautiful, independent, always smiling, jovial and full of life. After a few meetings, he realized that she too had her own set of problems with her in-laws, husband, sisters and all sort of relationships, but she had a way to deal with all this. She dealt with all the problems in her own smart way. One fine evening, she did not come for practice. The other evening, she was extremely silent, yet she was smiling but something was missing in her face. While leaving, they had a small talk and much too his surprise, she shared with him that she was very upset with her husband's all-time flirting attitude with a lot of their girlfriends. She was not asking for support, she did not even shed a tear, she was just plain upset and was looking for different solutions – this was so unlike Abha, who loved to crib and cry for every small-big issue.

There was a spark between Neeraj and Shiksha, which simply turned into a burning fire in no time. They spent more and more time together, and the more they knew about each other, the more they got attracted to each other. There was no looking back then. In spite of the fact that Shiksha's marriage was also not working, she was not ready to give up her marriage. She knew that her husband Rahul did love her a lot; it was just his habit to be over friendly with girls. And he was not ready to change this habit. Moreover, what would she tell their families? There was the usual social pressure associated with divorces that she was not prepared to take. Shiksha could not connect with her husband, the way she connected with Neeraj. Neeraj could not see Abha suffer even when he knew that there was nothing that could work between them.

It is a deadlock. And there are numerous such stories that exist in our urban modern lifestyle today. 'What really is different than how our older generations were? Every story is different. Every story has a lot of stress. Every story has a lot frustration. Every story seems to be a disaster. Why is our generation so confused about what they want? Are we not ready to compromise or are we not ready to share ourselves? Is it that we are too busy to think straight or are we too independent, liberal and modern?'

CONFLICT AND RESOLUTION

The thought of ending her life was not new to Amrita. She had serious suicidal thoughts in the past, but never really had the courage to do it. This time, it was different. She did not know whether she should call herself a whore or somebody who is trying to cope with the speed of life. In the last thirty days, she had gone out with two different men, both of them from different phases of her life, both of them with different tastes and both of them were crazy about her for different reasons. She had no clue if she loved even one of them or was all this just a rebound of her broken marriage.

At the age of thirty, after finally deciding to move out of her abusive and broken marriage, Amrita had no idea where her life was taking her. Five years of giving herself completely to John mentally, physically and spiritually, she now had nowhere to go, no place to look forward to. 'What had gone wrong?' she thought. 'I gave him all that I had; I loved him more than anybody has ever loved me. But still he had the need to go outside the marriage to meet his physical and emotional needs.'

John and Amrita fought with their families six years ago to get married to each other, which eventually happened on 19 October 2006. The day of her marriage was the happiest day of her life. She believed that she finally found her soul mate and that she was so lucky to have him in her life. Immediately after marriage she moved in to live with him, she understood all his problems. She understood when he said there could be no honeymoon because of the financial crunch. She understood when he had to spend late nights in office for the extra work. She understood when he wanted to spend boy's night out with his colleagues. She did her best to make him feel 'not bound' and free in spite of being married. She never really liked the way men in her office used to talk about how nagging their wives were and about how they felt so free when they were alone. She did not want to be one of them, so she chose to be an understanding wife. Little did she know that this was going to be so disastrous?

She knew that John had tried his level best to make Amrita comfortable with his friends. He wanted her to get drunk and enjoy the parties, to have her girlfriends and spend as much as time as he spends with his friends, to enjoy cricket and other sports as much as he did. She tried her best to be what he wanted her to be, but every time she made an effort, she felt that she was moving away from what she always wanted to be.

She had always thought that they would always make a perfect couple. She was an organized and loner kind of a person whereas he was a fun-loving and extrovert person. She thought that they would just be perfect for each other since she would bring in enough organization and meaning in his life and he would bring in enough fun and joy in her life. However, what happened was unexpected. After giving up trying to be what he wanted her to be, she started spending more and more time alone, writing songs and stories, painting, reading and taking care of her home. She thought that she was doing the right thing by giving him space to be himself and at the same time spending enough time by herself. He struggled for some time but eventually he too gave up trying to change her.

Slowly and gradually, so much of a distance was created between them that it became impossible for them to spend even half an hour together. There were no dinners together, no walks together, no fun together, only fights and more fights. Once when she realized this, she became hysterical and wanted to spend more time with him. Moreover, no matter what she did now, he could not like her for the person she is. With no physical intimacy and ever reducing emotional intimacy, they started living as two room-mates. There were only blames and complaints. He complained about how demanding she has become and she complained about he not being interested in her anymore. He wanted to be out of the house and be with his friends and she wanted to be with him. They were just tied in a relationship, which was empty and meaningless. They often got into physical fights; there were things around the house that were broken while fighting. He even got a hairline fracture on his fists after hitting into a wall; she got marks all over her face. Her ever shining, smiling face became dull and lifeless.

Three months ago when she found out about John's affair with one of his colleagues, her entire world collapsed around her. She wasn't really surprised; she knew that it was coming. She had nightmares about it. And eventually, now it was for real. An attractive, young and sexy colleague of his was somebody who understood his feelings, believed in his dreams, made him a Hero of her life. And here she was – his wife, who had turned into a nagging, suspicious, unattractive woman, who only knew how to blame her husband for leaving her alone all these years.

Not knowing what to do, after two months she moved out of the house to stay alone. She told her story to one of his colleagues – Sahil. This guy completely supported her and sympathized with her. She started liking this kind of importance. More she told him about her misery, more importance she got from him. In no time, she started flirting with him and started liking his company, finally there was somebody who could understand her, feel her emotions and sympathize with her. It was good. She already knew that he liked her and this was more than enough for her. He asked her out on one of the weekends; after hesitating a little, she said yes. They spent a wonderful time roaming around the malls and shopping places, had a yummy, romantic dinner in a restaurant. Before she even realized, they were holding hands and walking. She realized that she wanted to be close to him physically. It was just that she did not know whether it was right or not. For once, she wanted to lose herself and feel loved. She had been longing for a touch, a spark, that heavenly feeling of being close to somebody. He took no time in getting this and that night at his place, they made crazy, uncontrollable love to each other.

Two weeks ago, she met another guy, Sankalp while she was travelling in a train alone. He was a middle aged, handsome man who offered her some help. He was a therapist. She started telling him all about her marriage and how it ended, he gave her some knowledge about subconscious mind and how we make stories in our lives. She understood all that, but she was totally enchanted and impressed by this man's clarity of thoughts and maturity level. More she compared this man to John, more she got attracted towards him. They met a few more times, hanging out with each other, talking about their past, their present and their future plans. This guy too expressed his attraction towards her. He was successful in making her feel like a princess, in making her feel that she is an important part of his life, in making her feel that she is so special. She was very pleased with him to make her feel this way. He bought gifts for her – an iPad, Swarovski diamond earrings, a handbag from Bulchee. No matter how much she denied these gifts from him, she ended up accepting them. Hanging out with him eventually turned into late night talks, romantic dinners and making endless love to each other!

Just moving on the way life was taking her, she kept meeting both Sahil and Sankalp regularly. In no time, she realized that she was all the time talking to or spending time with one of these two men. She did not understand what really was happening to her. She definitely was happier now. She was doing things to impress both of them. 'Did she really love both of them? Is all this just a rebound? Does she really want to go ahead with these kinds of affairs?'

She wanted the answers but did not have the courage face the reality. She was happy and after all the pain and suffering and concluded in her mind, 'I definitely deserve to be happy.'

One fine day, she decided to join a gym and start working out the way she did before marriage. She went for a compulsory a health check-up and when she was asked about her last menses, she had no clue. That made her think and worry, 'Oh my god, when was it the last time!' She straightaway headed to the chemist to get a pack of pregnancy tests. And the result was a disaster – a positive. She went numb from head to toe. 'How did this happen? What was I thinking? How could I be so careless? What happens now? What about my baby?' Endless questions in her head and the worst one was 'Who is the father?' There was no way she could know that. She wanted to scream and cry but there were just no tears, no voice. She could not feel herself alive; she could not feel herself breathe. She hated herself, she felt like a whore, not even knowing who the father of her baby was.

For two days, she locked herself in her apartment. Did not go to work, did not take any calls, and did not meet anyone. She thought and thought, and after a long time, she was thinking and not cribbing. 'What have I turned my life into?' was the question reverberating in her head. 'Why do I need a man in my life to make me feel good?' She realized that since she was eighteen, she had been with one guy or the other. She was an attractive female and always attracted guys around her. Finally, she ended up getting married to John and depended totally on him to make her feel loved. When that failed, she depended on these men to make her feel good and important. 'Why? Why do I need a man to make me feel my beauty? Why do I need a man to show how special and a lovable person I am? Why can't I love myself, feel special for myself?'

This was a moment of transformation for her. She made up her mind to give up her self-pity and self-blame and take on the life with confidence. She promised herself never to seek sympathy from anybody. She made an agreement with herself to never blame, criticize or invalidate herself. She decided to live a life of dignity and high esteem. For the first time she felt, that it was not John, Sahil or Sankalp who was at fault. 'If I don't respect myself enough, nobody else ever will. If I don't believe in myself, nobody else ever will. If I make myself a sympathy figure, I can never have a high self-esteem. If I depend on other people to make me happy, I also give them the power to give me pain.'

Given this kind of a transformation, there was no reason for her to worry about anything. It was not a matter of concern whether she decided to give birth to this baby or not, whether she wanted to re-marry or not. Whatever decisions she would take, she would take it as a new person who was confident, had faith in herself, loved and respected herself to the core.

It was not a conflict with the world. It was a conflict with self. It is usually the conflict with oneself, which is the hardest to resolve. And once resolved we move one level up in our spiritual wellbeing. This is life.

FAT SHAME AND SKINNY SHAME

'Do you really have to eat cheese? Don't you see how much you are bulging from your hips?'

Shanaya was too tired of listening to this. Sometimes her boyfriend would say something about her diet and other times one of her friends or sisters would make her realize how fat she has become since last few months. She has always been heavy built, no matter how much she went to gym, dance classes or aerobics, her weight would never go down. Since her college days, she had been humiliated because of the way her figure is. She obviously looked a bit older than her age because of her size.

In spite of the fact that she was heavy, she loved eating. She couldn't resist food. She relished eating and she had a knack for different kinds of taste. Italian, Chinese, continental, Indian, Thai or any other cuisine, she loved it all. Though, she knew that she had to control her diet to look fab, she tried her best but she failed miserably almost every time.

She hated herself, her body, her looks, her liking towards food, everything. She remembered her mother saying, 'You better control your weight or else you will look ugly and fat.' That was the first time she thought the words fat and ugly are synonymous. And yes, they were. That is exactly what TV and magazine advertisements proved.

Depression can prove to be very harmful for a growing girl who is turning into a woman. She had found a way out of this depression. She used to exercise like crazy; she loved dancing and working out in the gym. She started doing this to get in shape, but she really started liking this. Now, gym was not a place where she felt miserable but it turned into a place where she could just lose herself and sweat out all her anger and depression.

She thought, 'how lucky are the people who can eat whatever they want and still stay thin without sweating in gym or dance.' There was one name that came striking to her every time she thought of such people – Nancy. Nancy was so lucky, she could have chocolates, cakes, ice-creams everything without feeling guilty at all, coz nothing changed her slim figure. 'How does this happen to a few people and cannot happen to her. Is it even possible that a girl like Nancy can ever feel pathetic and have low body image?' she wondered.

'Real women have real curves. I don't even know how any guy would find you even desirable with such a skinny flat figure.'

'Eat more bananas with milk, it will add to your body weight.'

'Did you try those new creams I got for you? They are supposed to add fat to your skin.'

Nancy ended up crying in a room because this was a millionth time she had heard her elder sister say this to her. Her friends said the same thing. 'Why am I so flat? Why can't I have a full figure?' She was really slim. She ate a lot; her appetite was as much as of a guy. However, it didn't affect her body at all. She loved eating just like Shanaya; she too took weight-gaining courses in gym and with nutritionist. She even applied all sort of oils to make her body look fuller and curvy than flat. Nothing really worked and she felt miserable about it.

Nancy too hated her body. She usually used to think, how lucky Shanaya is, at least she has good curves. What if she has a little fat on her belly and her hips, it makes her even more desirable.

'I don't understand why Shanaya keeps crying about her own body. She looks perfect. People say that she looks like perfect full figure,' thought Nancy.

On the other hand, Shanaya thought, 'Nancy is so crazy. Can't she see those models in TV; they all are skinny. I think she just doesn't understand how fortunate she is to have a body that doesn't gain weight at all. She will never have to worry about her weight.'

Nancy was talking to herself at the same time, 'Shanaya doesn't get that models look so artificial and look good only on the television. No guy really wants a size-zero girlfriend, they want a sexy girl with complete beauty.'

'Nancy feels pathetic about her body and I have no clue why. If a girl like her goes around the beach in a bikini, people are going to like her. If a girl like me goes around in a bikini, people will take offense in that. They will suggest me not to do something like this till she has a slimmer figure,' said Shanaya to herself.

'Shanaya doesn't know how much it pinches when people call me flat. When people say that I am not desirable, how rejected I feel at every comment of this kind,' thought Nancy.

Both Shanaya and Nancy had to work on their own body image. Nevertheless, both of them had to realize that this world is so full of confusion about what really is beautiful. They had to realize that beauty is what you define. Beauty is a combination of inner beauty, confidence and natural sex appeal. Moreover, it has got nothing to do with what media portrays or people believe. It has to come from inside of every person.

Fat shame exists and so does skinny shame. Both are equally painful and degrading. Both do the equal damage.

Pretty Faces Can Have Brains Too

It was her first day at office and Tanuja was already feeling weird. She was introduced to all her team members and obviously, she hardly remembered any names. All she noticed was that it was a very young team and comprised of mostly males in their late twenties. She was the only fresher and the youngest member of the team. Her team lead was an exciting fellow, charming and very helpful. So were the rest of the members of the team.

There were just two more ladies in the team – mid thirties, married with kids. She was quite excited to work for this company as a part of this team. She had always been a brilliant student, mostly among the toppers. Now she was in a huge product-based MNC working as Software Engineer. It looked like a very fun loving and yet hard working set of people.

FIRST PROJECT

Tanuja received her first project, which was to work on some shell scripts. She had never done scripting ever in her life. She had no idea where to start from, even after a quick ramp up from her lead. She asked for help from Rishi who sat in the next cubicle and he helped her very enthusiastically. There was a point of time where she felt that she was getting much more help than she asked for. She hesitatingly told Rishi that she could take it from here and would ask him if she needs more help. She finished the project on time and received quite an appreciation with an award.

FRIENDS AND MORE FRIENDS

Tanuja was very open and good in talking to people. She had the right modulation in her voice and she indeed was very charming. She had a lot of friends and in no time she made a lot of friends at workplace too. Some of them were from the team, others from the gym and few others from her dance team. Yes, she was also a dancer and had joined the dance team too.

FIRST PROSPECTIVE BOYFRIEND

Tanuja always attracted the attention of boys. She knew she is very pretty, much above average. However, she was very surprised the way boys were approaching her since she had joined this company. This place was definitely very short of girls, let alone pretty ones.

'How can a man who is married and has a kid come and flirt with me?' It was unbelievable for Tanuja. In her world, men who were married were supposed to be decent. This was the first myth broken. She understood men are always men, no matter at what stage of their lives.

One of the guys in her team just four years senior to her – Rajiv invited her for coffee. After a few coffee breaks with him, he told her that he liked her. Tanuja wasn't interested in a relationship, she simply wanted to have lots of friends and have fun in life. She was just out of a college time relationship and she wasn't ready for the next one. She told exactly this to Rajiv.

After that day, Rajiv became quite rude to her. He would ignore her for no reason, wouldn't even look at her or talk to her. It was very clear to her that it was a visible sign of so-called male ego. 'What an immature behaviour,' Tanuja thought.

FIRST REALITY OF HER JOB

Tanuja was working on yet another project, which was a getting a bit difficult for her to handle. She was a bit shy to ask for help and she definitely did not want to approach anyone until there was no way to do it herself. She looked for all solutions and finally started coding. After a week's effort of coding almost nine hours a day, she was ready to get her code and design to be reviewed. Unfortunately, her code had to be reviewed by her team lead and Rajiv. Couple of days later, Rajiv came to her desk with a very serious face.

'Tanuja, what were you thinking while creating a design of this kind?' asked Rajiv in a disappointed tone.

'What happened, Rajiv? What is wrong with it?' replied Tanuja surprised.

'Didn't you see other modules before designing this one? This is just not the way we work. You could have asked for help.'

'I am sorry, Rajiv. Just let me know what needs a change, I'll do it exactly the way you want,' said Tanuja.

'Okay, come and meet me post-lunch. We will discuss this in detail,' said Rajiv without looking at her in the eye.

During lunch time, Tanuja went to the ladies room in the cafeteria when she heard Rajiv's voice outside at the washing area. He was talking to somebody else.

'You know that new chick named Tanuja, she is such a pathetic programmer. I have no idea where do they hire the pretty-looking girls who have no brains at all. I am afraid we will have to handle her workload also. The other day only Rishi was telling me that she made Rishi waste almost half a day on those silly shell scripts. Such girls are only good as girlfriends and not as colleagues. Probably such girls should be hired only as a showpiece in the team for our entertainment and nothing else,' said Rajiv and then there was a roar of laughter.

Tanuja got her first ever blow on face.

SECOND REALITY OF HER INTERVIEW

Tanuja was extremely disturbed by what she heard in cafeteria. She just didn't know how would she take all this in a positive way. A showpiece for their entertainment – what the hell did he mean by that. I have to report this to somebody. She went and spoke to her team lead. Unaware of how to start the topic, she went and casually asked him, 'Ravi, how did I do in my technical interviews? I must have got the question about "virtual destructors" wrong.'

She had become quite comfortable with Ravi. He seemed to give her a good feedback and helped her understand things.

'Don't tell me you didn't even go and find out about the questions after the interview.' Ravi mocked. 'You got most of them wrong, but then a pretty girl like you doesn't have to answer the questions. You just have to smile at the interview panel,' said Ravi laughingly.

Tanuja just stared at him for a while. She didn't even believe this. How could I get most of the interview wrong and still get selected.

Looking at her face, Ravi immediately said, 'Hey, don't feel bad. I was just kidding. I don't mean it like that. I mean you did well but not exceptionally well. You definitely got the whole "doubly linked list" problem correct. And you know most of OS answers from you were bang on.'

Tanuja just smiled and she walked away. Unable to walk properly, she just went into the ladies room. She felt numb. She was hired for looking pretty. 'What is this? Some sort of joke that people were playing on her.' Feeling utterly alone and dejected, she lost all her confidence. She cried her heart out as much as she could.

FINAL BLOW

While she was crying sitting on the commode, she heard somebody talk outside. 'Yes, I know. She looks like a flirt too. Didn't you see how she was enjoying all the importance from Rishi, Abhay and other guys at the last month's dance party? A pretty girl like her would do things like that, what else do girls of this age do?' said one of her teammates.

'I think a lot of guys like Tanuja. She is beautiful, single and looks like more than available. Why won't guys pursue her?' said the other female.

This was just the right amount of blow that Tanuja was least expecting. Even the ladies in her team were unsupportive. What was she to do now? Her first instinct was to just quit this job and look for another one, but then who can guarantee that something like this will not happen in her next job.

THE COMEBACK

She cried, she thought, she worried about all this a lot. Finally, she decided to take it as a challenge. She was now determined to prove to every single person in her team that a fashionable girl like her with a pretty face could have brains too. She can handle her looks and her work in a way much better than anybody else. And now was the time to get back.

The very next day, she approached her manager to tell him that she wanted to work on a Java project. She knew it better than anything else and she would be able to perform much better in that. He asked her to give him some time so that he could find out where she could fit in.

She was now moved to work on Java. Right from the day one, she hit on all the architecture documents and every possible piece of code to understand exactly how these entire software modules were weaved into each other. She spent her nights and weekends working madly. There was nothing else on her mind than to prove that she was capable of doing this job. It was important for her to regain her confidence. She could not let this go. She could not let people relate to just her pretty face and not her brains.

Six months later, she was sent on an onsite project to work with the client because she became the sole point of contact for the clients. Since she was very capable of talking to people freely, she was the best person to communicate any issues on the calls. She knew the code in and out; she knew the product very well. She knew exactly what is needed to make this software work. Nobody could fix the bugs as fast as she could.

MUCH LATER IN LIFE

Thirteen years later, she was one of the managers in another MNC. She grew and grew because not only did she use her brains but also her beauty to influence people. As a manager of a twenty-seven-member team, when one day she gave the offer letter to a girl named Akriti just out of college – pretty and innocent face, she knew exactly what this girl would have to go through.

And then much worse happened to Akriti, Tanuja heard rumours in the team that Akriti was openly flirting with her team lead to get her way in the team. This was unacceptable to Tanuja and when she called Akriti in talk to her, it just took fifteen minutes for Akriti to start sobbing like a little child frustrated and convinced that her only talent is to look pretty.

A NEW BEGINNING

Tanuja knew this was happening all over the company. When young guys are asked to take interviews and decide whom to hire, they tend to prefer pretty girls that they would like to spend time with. It becomes a biased opinion. If the girl is really talented, she has to struggle to prove herself like Tanuja did or if the girl's talent is not in technology; she simply loses all her confidence trying to cope up with the tough world of technology and finally loses out to frustration and dejection.

This could not work for the company and definitely not for those girls. Tanuja being at a senior position now, decided to take this up, the first thing she did was to arrange for these corporate talks with the teams where she would bring up this topic very openly.

The corporate talk that she held on 'Hiring the right people,' she very clearly saw amusement in people's faces when she mentioned pretty girls. No, it wasn't funny. You have to hire people based on their capability and not their faces or bodies. Secondly, whoever is hired needs to be treated equally – not as a showpiece or an entertainment package.

This needed to be the guideline of every company and strictly followed, though deep down inside she knew it wasn't possible.

RE-DISCOVERING HERSELF

She stood in front of the mirror, naked and ran her hands over her breasts – they had never been this big and out of shape. Her eyes went down to her belly – oh, the stretch marks, it hurts so bad to see them. Her eyes were moist now, she turned a bit around and the stretch marks on her sides and hips were so visible. 'How the hell will I ever get rid of them? How will I ever wear sarees with this plump right here?' Alia thought while pinching the falling loose skin on her belly. She was crying bitterly now; her hair all messed up she just couldn't help but pull them. She pinched herself so bad on the tummy that she almost got blue bruises.

'Is he ever going to love me the same way? And why should I blame him, who would like to have sex with this gross body? Forget about the bikinis, I cannot even go around in shorts now?' thought Alia.

'Don't think this way, Alia. Look at your baby; isn't she the most beautiful princess in the world! What kind of mother you are, thinking of your lost figure when you have such precious gift in your life now?' thought Alia again.

Alia had her baby girl five months ago. This was her first pregnancy and she had no idea it will do this to her body. It was time for her to go back to work, but she simply didn't want to. These thoughts kept running in her head like a movie. It was the devil once reminding her of how pretty and gorgeous she looked earlier and now all her charm was lost – making her feel disgusted. Other times, it was the angel reminding her of her baby which was the amazing gift she has received from heaven – making her feel guilty about thinking about her body instead of her baby. It was tennis game all throughout the day, whenever she was alone.

'C'mon Alia, it is just a matter of one night. Can't Abhay take care of the baby? Tina and Rosie are also coming; it'll be fun. It has been ages since we had a girl's night out yaa. Come dear, it won't be fun without you,' said Tanya – one of Alia's friends.

'No Tanya, you know Abhay is already so tired with the hectic schedule at work, he really cannot handle the baby. You girls carry on; I'll join you the next time. Moreover, I am so tired with all the work that I really don't have the energy to go,' said Alia.

'Tanya won't understand. It is not that I cannot come for the night out, but seriously what would I wear? I don't want to be an odd one out; these girls would be all nicely dressed up in their skirts, shorts or dresses. None of my old dresses fit me now and with this huge jiggly tummy, whatever I wear is going to make me look like a fatso.

Imagine the guys hitting on these girls and I would be sitting in one corner sipping fruit juice. 'Has she forgotten that I am feeding the baby, I am off vodka and tequila?' wondered Alia. This wasn't the first time her girlfriends had tried to get her out of her home and baby work, but she simply wouldn't step out of her house because she was ashamed of how she looked now.

'If you are so worried about the stretch marks, go join a gym sweetheart. Unless, you start working out how do you expect yourself to get back in shape,' said Abhay tired of listening to her endless complaints about her weight gain.

'Do you know how much work it is with the baby? Try staying at home with her for a day, you will know. Where on earth do I have time for gym? If you have so many problems with my body, go find another wife for yourself,' screamed Alia at the top of her voice crying bitterly.

'Alia, I am so tired of your complaints. Either stop complaining or do something about it. It has just been five months, give yourself some time.' Abhay tried to pacify her biting his own anger and frustration.

'I had to give up my job, Abhay. I cannot go out with my friends. I cannot drink. I cannot dance. I don't feel confident even in a pair of jeans. Last week I went out to buy groceries and I felt every person was staring at my tummy as though everybody out there could see my body covered with stretch marks. I hate myself. I cannot take it anymore. I just want to die,' she said, crying bitterly.

'C'mon darling, don't say that. You know I love you. You are the mother of my daughter. Your major focus should be well-being of our baby; don't think so much about your body. You look perfect. Please don't say such negative things about yourself; it hurts me too,' said Abhay taking Alia in his arms.

She felt better and Abhay left for work. While she was feeding the baby, she remembered the first time she had done that in the hospital. Nurse taught her how to hold the baby comfortably, how to make sure that all the milk goes in her mouth. And the moment baby took her milk; it was a feeling so divine. She almost cried with joy looking at her baby happily sucking on her nipples. She could make out the feeling of satisfaction on baby's face. She could just hold the baby to her breast forever and ever. 'O, what a beautiful gift nature has given me,' she thought.

'I am going to cover up all the mirrors in the house. No more mirrors, no more stares at my ugly body. No more negativity about it. I can go to the gym downstairs for an hour while maid is here for the baby; it won't hurt anybody.' Well-determined Alia decided.

Baby was sleeping peacefully in her bed. Alia looked at those tiny little eyes closed so peacefully, those half open little lips, her cute hands and legs and all she felt was pride. 'My daughter is just beautiful. She is a perfect baby. I wonder what she would be dreaming about. Oh, they say that little babies dream of their past life. What would she be in her past life? Where did I get her from?

Whoever she might be, I know I am very lucky to have her,' thought Alia happily as a proud mother.

Now was the time to hit the gym. 'Seriously, I almost feel like fainting when I see the treadmill,' thought Alia and then she thought of her ugly body. She was suddenly motivated to go. She ran for about ten minutes; she had been a good runner since her school days but now such a long break had made her lose all the stamina. She was determined to build up the stamina again, she ran for another ten minutes and then another. Now, she absolutely had no energy to run more. She did cycle for ten more minutes and she decided that it was enough for the first day.

As she was coming out of the gym, she met Aunt Sharma – an elderly lady in her society. 'So, I see you are coming to the gym now. Is it losing all this pregnancy weight gain?'

'No Aunty, not just that; I also want to regain my stamina,' said Alia, trying to act comfortable about her body.

'Stamina and all is ok; you don't have to run in Olympics. But you should definitely do something about the weight and all this plump loose skin; you know it can be very stubborn. It doesn't go away no matter how much you run or cycle,' said Aunty touching her sensitive nerve.

'It is fine Aunty. I can only try to reduce, rest all depends,' said Alia, now almost in a hurry to leave as soon as possible.

'My daughter-in-law went to VLCC for weight-loss sessions, those helped her greatly. You know these days various surgeries are also possible to let go of this stubborn loose skin. It doesn't even leave a scar. In our days, only rich models and actress could afford such procedures; but now it is really cheap, just for a lakh of rupees you can rid of all the stretch marks and jiggly skin,' continued Aunty.

'Okay Aunty, I'll talk to you later. I have left baby since a long time. I have to rush,' said Alia, hurriedly, irritated by Aunty's lecture.

As soon as she came in her apartment, she rushed to the mirror. Yes, all the mirrors were covered but not anymore. She looked at her body and started crying again.

'Have you totally lost your mind? Surgery? Surgeries are done, when there is something wrong with the body, not because you want to be thin.' Abhay almost shouted angrily.

'Sharma Aunty suggested me, so I just called up VLCC and other clinics. It is really cheap Abhay, we can afford it. Look, it has been a month since I am going to the gym; it is not helping. I really want to look hot and sexy like I looked two years back, Abhay. It is very important for me,' said Alia, tears rolling down her eyes.

'It is not about the money, Alia. Of course, we can afford it. But you have to understand that your body is not going to be hot and sexy all throughout your life. Someday you will be sixty years old with wrinkles on your face, will you get another surgery done for that? This is all a part of growing up. Good looks aren't the only important thing in the world. Focus on your talents; I have never come across a better web designer than you. If you don't want to join a job, take up freelancing; I can get you the contacts. But get your mind off looking good, there are much better things in the world to take care of,' explained Abhay.

'Please Abhay, I will do whatever you say – freelancing or job; but before stepping out of the house, I have to feel confident about how I look,' begged Alia.

'You have totally lost your mind, Alia. I wish I could make you see how much more you are for me and for this world than just a hot and sexy body. Nobody cares Alia; people who love you are still there for you. And if you insist on it so much, you can go for it but on one condition – you have to go for some counselling sessions and then if you still feel that you need the surgery, I won't say no,' said Abhay, giving up the argument.

'Counselling? For god's sake Abhay, I am not mad. But fine, if this is your condition; I will go for counselling sessions and after that I am directly going to VLCC to get this plump skin cut off from my body,' irritated Alia slammed the door behind her.

'Tell me about your mother, how she looked like?' asked the counsellor

'She was very pretty at least that's what my father tells me till she had me and my brother. I have seen her pictures too; she was far prettier than I am. Or was. She used to tell me that she has become "fat and ugly" now. When all of us used to have aloo paranthas with lots of butter on it, she used to have some sprouts or corn flakes. She never ate anything outside, always went for regular walks and exercises, still she never lost any weight,' explained Alia.

This was her second counselling session and in spite of her initial hiccups, she quite liked it. After ages, she had somebody to open her heart out to. And she was glad that her counsellor wasn't judging her; she simply listened and absorbed all that Alia had to say.

'Fat and ugly? Do you think whoever is fat is always ugly?' asked the counsellor in a neutral tone.

'No, not always. I don't know, I am not sure; all I know is that I have become fat and I look quite ugly.' Alia was confused now.

And so many more sessions continued....

Dear Mom,

I remember that you were my idol when I was a little girl. You were the definition of beauty for me. I considered myself so lucky to be born to you, coz I knew that I am going to grow up pretty like you. I never understood why you had lived on corn flakes and why you stopped having ice-creams with us. There was nothing wrong with you. I remember, I used to feel bad to see you upset, when Dad and Granny scolded you for eating outside. I remember how we used to order Chinese food and you still had dal and chawal. I remember your moist eyes, Mom!

Then one day when you were too angry, you said that dad doesn't love you anymore because you didn't deserve to be loved. And when I asked why, you said because you had become fat and ugly. Mom, since then for me fat always meant ugly. I was deeply scared to get married to somebody and to have babies, to be called fat and ugly. I learnt very early in life that I wouldn't deserve to be loved if I become fat and ugly. I realized that there is no point of my education, my job, my talent or qualification, if I was fat and ugly.

Why did you do this to yourself, Maa? It affected me too deeply. Only if you could stand up to dad and tell him that if he loved only your body, he didn't deserve you.

You are and you always will be what I saw you initially – a perfect epitome of beauty and no amount of fat or stretch marks or wrinkles can ever take that away from you because you are beautiful person inside. Your love, your affection and your care for people made you beautiful. Your kindness to strangers and your ever-smiling face is your beauty. I was right Maa, when I was a little girl – you are a perfect beauty; beauty of a Goddess.

Love you Maa.

Alia read out this mail to Abhay just after she had sent it. Abhay smiled and hugged her. He instantly knew that he had his wife back, and that now he was looking at the mother of his child.

'I am proud of you, Alia. I love you so much for this. Never again talk to me about your ugly body, because you are the prettiest girl on earth. I know it and now you know it too,' said Abhay, kissing her gently.

'Thank you Abhay,' Alia could only say this when he held her close pressed his lips against hers in a deep kiss.

They made love that night and Alia was herself; the same sexy, hot girl in the bed with her true love. She never thought about the loose jiggly skin on her body, never did she care about her body covered in stretch marks. She knew that her beauty was her pure heart, her amazing talents, her self-confidence and her self-respect.

She still went to the gym only to up her stamina and flexibility and to stay fit. Aunt Sharma never bothered her with any more suggestions. She made it a point to go out for movies and girls night outs once every month. She still wore beautiful dresses and danced in them till she got tired. She was happy with herself and the way she looked. She started freelancing web designs while taking care of the baby and now was earning more than her husband. Everything fell right in place for Alia once she got her body image right.

A Special Dinner

Suparna was so happy today. She could not entrust her cook today; she had to make the dinner herself and make it really good. Someone special was coming for dinner today, that's what Akshay had said casually over breakfast. There was still so much work to be done; only Kadhai Paneer was partially ready, the whole menu was there in front of her.

Akshay, her son was now thirty-two and still unmarried. Relatives were already asking and so were the neighbours but more than that she and her husband Amit were getting really old. She desperately wanted to play with her grandchildren before she got too old to do that. But Akshay had always been denying any offers that came for him.

A year ago, they had to suffer so much of embarrassment when they had a meeting scheduled with Mrs Sharma's niece. Akshay refused to show up for the meeting; he switched off his phone. Suparna had no idea what to tell the guests even after multiple rounds of tea. It was utterly embarrassing. Akshay did not come back home till past midnight, much after the guests had left.

'I do not want to get married. Why can't both of you just leave me alone?' That's all he had said before banging the door in anger.

Next day morning, Akshay came to his mom with a remorseful face, 'Sorry Ma, I shouldn't have shouted on you. But seriously, if you force me into this marriage thing, it will not work for me at all.'

'But beta, your age..'

'Mom, what age? I have to feel comfortable to get married. It is the most important relationship of anybody's life. I cannot just spend my life with anybody. I want my wife to be special and I want to choose her myself. I believe in God, Ma. When time comes, I will meet her and you will be the first person to know about it. That is my promise; now please promise me that you will stop looking for a partner for me.'

Suparna trusted her son. With tears in her eyes, she hugged her son and promised him never initiate this talk about marriage till he himself was interested. Since then, Suparna and Amit never persuaded him to get married. But that did not mean that they stopped getting worried about it. In her everyday prayers, she would just ask for one thing – a daughter-in-law. Amit had totally withdrawn himself from all family matters after that day. Apart from his prayers, walk, pranayama, regular tea and three meals of a day, there was nothing else in his life. Though Suparna knew that Amit was also very worried about his son, but he hardly ever shared his emotions with her.

She was now sweating due to the heat in the kitchen. Everything had to be perfect today. She took out her latest dinner set and laid it on the table, and again went running to the kitchen to have a look at suji ka halwa. 'Finally, he has decided to get married. He has everything – good height, education with great grades, a stable job and thanks Lord for all that,' she thought. The only part missing in her life would also get filled in now. Today was finally the end of all their worries. But she really had to hurry up. Akshay had said that they would be home after 7 from work. Only two hours were left and so much had to be done.

'Oh, what should I wear? I should have applied henna today, only if Akshay had told me earlier. My greys would show, but how does it matter. I am going to be a mother-in-law, I should look like one,' thought Suparna. She couldn't help wondering what the girl would be like. Well, it was only a matter of couple of hours.

It was 7 pm; they would be at the door anytime now. Suparna made sure that everything was perfectly ready and Amit was dressed up too. She quickly wore her new pink-coloured saree with golden border matched with her gold jhumkis and pink bangles. She wondered if she was over-doing her dress-up, after all she is supposed to look a mother-in-law now. Well, it was a special evening and she wanted to dress up nicely and so she did.

At7:40 pm and the doorbell rang; Suparna rushed to the door and noticed for the first time that it was raining heavily. As soon as she opened the door, she saw Akshay with a doll-like pretty girl dressed in a blue jeans and red flary top. She was wearing black boots and some trinkets on the wrist. Suparna was a bit surprised; she wasn't expecting this but she greeted both of them inside. She saw Akshay signal her and she bent down to touch her and Amit's feet. Her black-coloured hair with highlights of brown was accentuating her pretty face cut. Her long earrings seemed to get mixed up in her hair. Suparna couldn't help but notice the innocence in her eyes. In spite of a butterfly tattoo on her arm, she looked very pure.

'Ma, this is my friend Tina. Tina, meet my Mom and Dad,' Akshay broke the silence and Tina folded her hands to greet both the elders.

'Come beta, please come and have a seat. I didn't realize it is cold outside, shall I make some tea or coffee now or would you like it later?' offered Suparna

'Aunty, it is fine. Please sit, we can have tea later,' replied Tina in her melodious voice.

Suparna liked her child-like voice. She sat down next to Tina and realized that the girl was wearing a floral mist fragrance.

'Aunty, I am really sorry to have come in this attire. Akshay invited me today morning only, by then I was already at work. Because of rain and traffic, it was impossible for me to go and change. Please don't mind it, Aunty. I definitely would have taken care of it, if I could,' said Tina and she really looked worried and sorry.

Suparna and Amit couldn't help but smile at her innocence. The more she talked, more Suparna liked her. Akshay was smiling too, that radiant smile of his that Suparna was dying to see since a long time.

'It is fine, beta. There is no problem at all. You look lovely.'

'Mom, she was planning to go home at 6 and dress up in a saree and come here. She wouldn't have reached before 9'o clock. It took me some time to convince her to just come over. She was too worried about what kind of perception will it give. I told her that my Ma and Paa are not from the eighteenth century,' Akshay said with a laugh.

Suparna was surprised to see him talk so much. He usually was very quiet at home and would mind his own business most of the times. Today, he looked different – dynamic and energetic. She could see how desperately he wanted us to like and approve of Tina.

The evening went on and they came to know more and more about Tina. She liked to go to gym regularly and that is where Akshay met her six months ago. She liked to dance dancing and play tennis. She lived with her sister in Bangalore and worked for an MNC as a Manager. She was four years younger than Akshay, but she definitely looked like twenty. She was outgoing and had a lot of friends.

Suparna realized that Tina talked so much but she never once mentioned her family except for her sister. Over the dinner table, Amit asked, 'Beta, what about your parents? Where do they stay?'

Tina's smile suddenly disappeared and Akshay put up a tensed expression too, which scared Suparna. She wondered if everything would be okay with the family.

'Uncle, Aunty, I know this is my first meeting with both of you and I know that questions about my family will be asked. Though, I want to tell you every bit of truth I really don't want you to judge me or my background without knowing me completely.'

Suddenly, the environment of house turned from happy to tense. Suparna and Amit looked at each other and then at Akshay. He had reassuring look in his eyes.

'I was born in Mumbai in one of the famous red-alert areas of the city. My mother was a prostitute and she had a very close affair with my father. My father was so much in love with her that he wanted to marry her, but did not have guts to stand up against his family and take a stand to marry a prostitute.'

Suparna's feet just froze to the ground as she heard the story. She couldn't move a muscle and did not know what she felt. A thousand thoughts ran in her mind: 'What will the people say? Is this girl really decent? What will I say during the marriage about this girl's background?'

'Before my father got married to another woman, I was born. He decided to adopt me but he had to convince his would-be wife first. This was a difficult situation for him because the woman he got married did not accept the situation nicely. My mother, on the other hand, did not want me to grow up in that environment, so she asked my father to take me away with him at any cost. He did so, but his wife did not agree to keep me in the same home as her own daughter. I studied in a boarding school and my father did as much as he could to give me a quality education. I used to visit them and my half-sister during my vacations and otherwise. I got really close to my sister Ananya, though my step-mother did not like it. We have been best of friends since ever and that is the reason why my step-mother has softened towards me now. I have visited my mother in Mumbai only a few times before she passed away couple of years ago,' said Tina with strong determination in her tearful eyes.

Suparna couldn't control her tears as well and she noticed Amit's look get really soft listening to all this. Akshay was continuously looking at Tina holding her hand to give her all the moral support that he could.

'You might feel that I was born to a less person, a person who doesn't deserve to be respected. All I can say about my mother is she kept me away from her because she did not want me to even slightly get affected by her life.

She loved me, she wrote letters to me, she craved to see me, to touch me and to hug me, but she sacrificed her motherhood only for my sake. And today I have a Master's degree and I work for the world's best company as a Manager. I know where ever she is, she would be proud of me and that is all that matters to me.'

'My father did all that he could for me, but he could not stand up to his family for me or my mother, yet he provided for all my financial needs if not love. The only love that I have received in my life is from my sister Ananya and then from your son. He means the world to me; he accepted me knowing all about me and told me to tell you all the truth the first time I meet you.'

She was sobbing like a child now. Her pure innocent eyes were filled with tears but strength in them still showed.

'Aunty, it is up to you to accept me or not, but as far as I have heard of this family, I know that this family can give me all the love I have missed in my life. And that is all that means to me.'

Suparna couldn't take it anymore; she just got up from her chair and hugged this little girl. She had never seen such a strong, brave and truthful girl. No matter what her family background is, she knew that this girl will make the perfect daughter-in-law to them and a perfect wife to her son. And before she knew Akshay and Amit were also wiping their eyes and she knew that this was an instant family connection.

STRUGGLE TO LOVE AGAIN

N atasha was deep in her thoughts after meeting Vishal. 'Was Vishal really proposing to me or was it all just made up,' she wondered.

It's been eight months since she was back from New Zealand and filed her divorce. Six months, since she had been single. 'It feels relieved to go back to the single life after being married for three years. Marriage was such a stress. No more marriage; I am happy the way I am. I'll be earning for myself, spending on myself and no worries in life. I have had enough of stress in three years for an entire lifetime.'

Natasha reminisced the day she first came to know that Abhay's family was interested in her. Abhay – Bhatia Uncle's son and her ex-husband came from a very hi-fi family. They wore branded clothes and went for international vacations. I had not even seen him since five years then, but still it was better than a typical arranged marriage. It was the best available option then. Best available option? What was I thinking; marriage is not about available options. Marriage is about love... which I and Abhay got over in a couple of years. And he felt that love for her.... Even at this thought, she felt her blood boiling. No, I have to focus on future, my future. There is no looking back. There is no Abhay and no one called Nancy in my life. There is only peace, compassion and love around me. There is no place for double standards, back stabbing, jealousy and hatred now.'

Eight long months filled with therapy sessions and interesting hobby classes; only to get over the trauma and rejection of her marriage. Vishal was her Salsa dance partner. She had always loved salsa, those graceful moves and those amazing lifts. It made her feel special. It made her feel worthy to be looked into the eye, to be smiled at and to be lifted.

'How about a long drive today evening?' offered Vishal.

'Long drive, wow! It has been ages. But will that be the right thing to do, going out with Vishal so late night? 'Chuck it, Natasha. Do as your heart say,' a voice inside her head said.

'Ok, let's go,' said Natasha timidly.

They sped down the Mysore road.

'I and Abhay stopped going for long drives also, after she came in. In fact, we stopped doing all those activities together that we used to. No long drives, no walks, no dinners together, no swimming, no dance sessions, no gym workout. It felt like we suddenly became strangers living in the same house,' Natasha said.

Vishal pulled over the car, turned to see tears in her eyes. He took her face in his hands. 'You are the most beautiful person in the world. He was jerk to not see that and take you for granted this way. You deserve to be a princess.'

'Don't say that, Vishal. It makes me feel... artificial. I am not begging for sympathy and kind words. I want to be strong. I want to believe it in me that I deserve to be loved,' she was almost sobbing now.

He kissed her forehead. 'You will know what you deserve and you'll be surprised at how much you have been denying yourself.'

'I wish I get amnesia and I forget last three years of my life. I go back to the time when I was twenty-four years of age, completely enjoying my life,' she said with a smile but the smile disappeared as soon as it came. 'I don't know what wrong did I do? Was I supposed to give him more expensive gifts? Was I supposed to serve him more? Was I supposed to be more liberal? Where did I fail as a wife? Why did he even need another woman to support him?' She was now thinking aloud. These were the same questions that had been giving her sleepless nights.

'Do you really want amnesia? People say that it usually happens with a trauma in the head. Fancy an accident?' He winked at her.

She smiled back. 'You are crazy.'

'Yes, I am. I am crazy for you.' He gave a look that gave her goose bumps.

'Stop it, Vishal. You are not starting it again.'

'You can't get down from this car. So, now I can kidnap you and even take advantage of you,' he laughed.

Vishal did this quite often and Natasha always took it as a joke. She knew that he had feelings for her, but her mind was so full that she could not afford to think about Vishal. He made her feel special and needed.

It was 7 am, when Natasha was getting ready for her office and felt extremely sad because she missed her long beautiful hair. A year ago, she had the most beautiful hair, long and thick straight up to waist. Looking at herself in the mirror, she remembered that dreadful day when she chopped her hair off. She had found some letters and emails of Nancy in Abhay's office. They called each other 'Sweetu and Bebu.' They went out for movies and shopping together. The iPad 3 and Galaxy S3 that Nancy carried was gifted by Abhay. Every night when Abhay was not home, he was with her. And they had incredible sex. Natasha did some more spying after she found those letters and she figured that this had been going on since last one year.

Nancy was an old friend of Abhay. They knew each other since the early days of their work life. When Natasha got married to Abhay, Nancy was a great support for her. She had left for US a week after they got married and came back New Zealand after two years of their marriage and everything changed. Natasha did everything she could to be real friends with Nancy. They went for endless shopping together, girl's night-outs and gossips. But deep down inside, Natasha was a little insecure because Abhay and Nancy were too important for each other. They met each other in office, yet she would talk to him for hours on phone after he is home. Sometimes they would start chatting late in the night. *There are supposed to be boundaries, after marriage.*

Natasha was getting killed from inside. Slowly and gradually, Abhay started spending much more time than usual at work. They stopped having sex altogether. The fights and arguments kept increasing. Natasha complained that Abhay was spending too much time with Nancy and not at home, which he completely denied. Life became way too stressful for both of them. Natasha tried to talk to Nancy about all this and she also started avoiding this topic after a couple of heated discussions. Natasha was left all alone and she knew that something was not right. So Natasha did some spying.

'I was right about them. They are having a secret affair. Why did he get married to me then, he could have married her? Why did he have to spoil my life?' screamed Natasha in desperate anger. She felt insulted, cheated and used. Her tears wouldn't stop. She called up Abhay right then, shouted at him the way she had never imagined. She blamed him for using her and accused him of cheating her. She was screaming and crying.

'I still love you Natu; please don't be so angry. I am sorry that it hurt you so much but sex was only once and that was a weak moment. I don't intend to leave you. I and Nancy are only good friends and nothing else. Sex just happened; we were so drunk after that party... I am sorry Natu.' Abhay had tried to console her. *'Sex just happened. Is it that simple? He just calls her Sweetu and Bebu because she is a close friend. I am not taking this bullshit,' she thought angrily.*

Abhay was completely indifferent towards her as though all this was only a drama. He did not think it was a big deal. Later, he apologized saying that he would *try* to keep a distance with Nancy. *Try, really try?*

Her first instinct was to chop off her hair. She wanted to change herself into somebody who is not so naïve and won't allow herself to be used again. She chopped her hair off, to above the shoulders. She went and got a tattoo made on her ankle. She got drunk that night. Insulted, humiliated and cheated, she simply did not know what was happening to her. She checked her mobile and it had close to hundred missed calls and messages. She did not care and went to a friend's place and spent the night there.

All this was enough for Natasha. The next day she took her bags and came to India telling Abhay that she wanted some time to think. Without letting him know, her lawyer sent him the divorce papers. It wasn't easy. Abhay begged and cried for her to come back. But she had enough. For an entire one year, they kept her in dark, told so many lies, and backstabbed her. When she finally found out, he said that he would try to keep a distance with her?

'*Nobody knows how it feels to be taken for granted and backstabbed by both your husband and best friend. How it feels to be so lonely that you have nobody to talk to? How it feels to be lied to? How it feels to wait for somebody all day only to find out that he is with another woman – your best friend? No, I could never give him a second chance and I could never forgive him. I have never hated anybody so much in my life as much as I hate both of them. No, I am not ready to live in that hell anymore. I don't want to be suspicious wife. This marriage was over.*'

Next morning, Natasha thought of Vishal and smiled. She felt like meeting him right away. The dance session was in the evening and she knew it'll be tough to wait till then. 'Am I falling in love all over again? No, I guess I am just enjoying being needed and feeling important. It is nothing else.' she wondered, dismissing the first thought.

The evening comes. 'O my god, I love the way he stared into my eyes while dancing and the smile. It is so killing,' she couldn't deny the fact that she had a little something for him.

Evening turned darker and Vishal dropped her home. Almost impulsively, Natasha invited him for coffee. Surprised at the invitation, he saw no reason to refuse. '*Why coffee? What's wrong with me?* 'she thought, surprised at her own invitation. They both came over to her apartment, she prepared coffee and as they sat in the balcony sipping slowly, when Vishal said, 'You cannot deny that I love you and you like the fact that I do.' He smiled.

Even when Natasha was about to say something funny, the seriousness of his intense eyes stopped her. '*He really does mean it.*' Completely at loss of words, she walked away from him. He followed her 'I understand that you are going through a tough time. Trying to heal yourself. But life has to go on. You know I have real feelings for you. I want to get married and have a family with you. You are just the way a woman is supposed to be. Perfect for me!' said Vishal almost whispering. He was so close to her that she could almost feel his warm breath on her face. She could feel her heartbeat rising and her stomach tightening. '*He is going to kiss me! Kiss me, Vishal please. I so wanted to be loved.*' He kissed her almost instantly as if reading her thoughts. And it felt like heaven. It had been so long since she got a loving kiss. 'I love you Natasha and I promise you that I will never ever leave you and take you for granted,' whispered Vishal in her ears.

'*No, he cannot be saying that.*' She pushed him away almost instantly. 'Please Vishal, don't make promises. Don't say things that you don't mean. Don't take oaths that you will simply forget and move on.' Natasha was almost shouting now. She turned to hide her tears.

'I am sorry, Natasha. I didn't mean to hurt you. I was just saying what I really feel for you. Please understand...'

'Abhay said all this to me on the day of our marriage and two years later he was probably saying this to Nancy,' said Natasha in such a cold voice that Vishal almost felt a shiver.

'C'mon Natasha, you cannot compare everything with Abhay. For god's sake, I am not a bastard like him,' shouted Vishal, almost irritated.

'Please leave Vishal. I don't think we are in a right mind to talk about anything right now,' says Natasha dismissing him.

'Well, yeah right. This is your way of dealing with a situation. Grow up, Natasha. It has been eight months, when will you get over him? I cannot wait for you forever.' He left slamming the door behind him.

'He is serious about me. But how can he expect me to just for forget everything in just eight months. Why is he reacting as if the world is on fire and I have to say a yes to him right now?'

Sleep was away from her this night. *'Am I on a rebound? Am I taking him for granted? He had been with me all throughout. He knows everything. He has put up with me through all my crying sessions and sent flowers and chocolates for me whenever I seem even slightly upset. And what did I do for him? Completely rejected him when he was so romantically opening his feelings for me and compared him with Abhay! I must be crazy. O god, I must apologize. I must tell him that I may not be ready for a relationship* but I do love him. I am trying to come out of this mess as soon as possible and it won't take very long. Please Vishal, stay with me.'

She had to talk to him today after the session. She had to set it right, no matter how much of an effort it takes. She would do it. 'I can do it. I can set it right. I have hurt him so much.'

After the dance session, Natasha requested him to stay over for some time in the studio. He agreed reluctantly. 'I am so sorry, Vishal. I shouldn't have reacted that way. I don't know why is it so difficult for me to move on? I am trying my best. I know you feel for me. I also want to be in love again. Just give me some time, Vishal. Please don't be so indifferent to me, you are the only one with me right now,' said Natasha sobbing.

'Do you still love Abhay?,' said Vishal.

'No, I don't. He has hurt me. I hate him from the very core of my heart,' said Natasha disbelieving that he actually asked this.

'You have to get over this hate. This hatred is occupying your heart so much that there is no place for love and for me.'

'How do I do that? I am doing all that I can.'

'Forgive him. Let me take you to another world now – world of your subconscious!'

She knew that he is a trained hypnotherapist. *He wants to do this now.*

'Just trust me, okay?' Said Vishal

She nodded obediently. She has to trust him. There is no other choice. She went and sat comfortably on the couch. He took her down under hypnosis and once she was safe there, he asked her to get Abhay and Nancy in front of her and say all that she wanted. She screamed and shouted at them, blamed them and accused them. She kept screaming for forty minutes and then she kept weeping for half an hour. Finally, when she came out of hypnosis and she felt lighter in her head and sleepy. It was as if somebody had taken a big burden off her shoulders and her mind.

She slept very peacefully that night almost for ten hours straight. In the morning when she woke up, she just wanted to stay in the bed the whole day, listen to music, read some books and be herself like the old days. She was finally free. The thought of Abhay and Nancy did not come to her mind for the whole day. She could not wait to go and tell this to Vishal and thank him for this.

That evening, Vishal and Natasha went out for dinner.

'Guess what, I spent the most peaceful day of last two years. I was me after so long,' said Natasha delighted and happy.

'I am glad you feel so relieved,' said Vishal casually.

It was like all new life for her. There was no hatred and she felt lighter than ever. There was only happiness and love around. Vishal came to her apartment and she realized how badly she wanted to kiss him. She could not let him go now. She was ready to fall in love once again and to make crazy, passionate love to him.

'I love you, Vishal. Thank you so much. I could have never done this on my own. You know you are a life saver now,' said Natasha winking at him.

'So since I saved your life, do I get a total right on you now?'

She laughed. 'Yes, my sweetheart. You do. I am all yours, do whatever you want,' her seductive voice took complete control of him. He kissed her passionately. She felt him and his love. Drowning in this love and trusting this man to the core, she gave in. She let herself be worshipped that night and for the rest of her life. She felt nothing less than a Goddess now. Finally her soul was at peace and in love.

THE HOME-MAKER

'Yaa right, that's what I want – a break from work,' Maya thought. After a long time, she would have all the time in the world for herself. Her daughter was going out for a school sports camp for an inter-school athletics competition. Her husband was away on an official tour. Her recent guests (her cousins) had also left eventually. The next day was Saturday and she was already making plans for it. It had been a long time since she was so excited for the weekend.

She decided she would get up really late, cook something really nice for herself. She planned to spend the whole day watching movies. She had the Blu-ray print of all eight Harry Potter movies, never had time to watch them in one go. She loved Harry Potter, because she believed in powers, in magic and in magic wands. 'Wow, two days full of Harry Potter!' she thought excitedly. She got some potato chips, popcorn, juice, Maggi and was all set to have Harry Potter marathon over the weekend – all alone.

Maya slept most peacefully on Friday night after seeing off her daughter at the railway station. She was worried about her teenage daughter, Sia. But she also knew that Sia was exceptionally good at athletics and it would be so unfair for Maya to stop her daughter's aspirations for her own inauthentic fears. Sia had always been truthful to Maya and Maya knew this really well. Never once, Sia tried to hide anything from her mom, not even when she had her first kiss. Maya knew she could trust her daughter. Once she reached home and reminded herself about the fun-filled weekend she will have, she was over her worries about Sia in no time.

Saturday morning came; it was 7:30 am when her phone rang. Maya received the call and it turned out to be her maid, who had called to inform her of the leave that she was taking. Disappointed Maya relaxed herself; it's just a two-hour job to clean up the house. 'I'll be done with it by 10 am and then I can start the movie marathon with my breakfast.' She called up Sia and her husband to know if everything is okay with them. Then she started cleaning up the utensils. It was almost 9:30 am, when she was almost done with the work. Just then, her phone rang again. This time, it was her brother in law. He just told her that they were coming for some wedding to her city and would like to visit them and stay for the weekend. Shocked Maya told him that her husband wasn't home, but like a good host she welcomed them to come over.

'Yes, we'll come over Bhabhi. We'll be there by 1 pm and have the lunch with you,' her brother in law said and hung up. She informed her husband of the plans, and he too decided to return on Saturday night, since his brother's family was visiting. Drained were all her plans of having the weekend to herself!

She just stood in front of mirror unable to control her tears. And before she even realized, she is already sobbing like a baby. Just one day she wanted for herself. Just one day, when she didn't have to cook for everybody and eat the leftovers herself; just one day when she could wake up really late; just one day when she could be happy with the house all messed; just one day when she could be herself. No, but that one day was not today. She tried explaining this to Rajiv multiple times, all that she got was 'What do you do the whole day? Just sleep, right? Do you know how much pressure boss gives me daily? And you only have to cook and clean, how much is it really?' She didn't have an answer to that.

Last weekend, Rajiv came back late from work and told her that he would have food at office itself. She didn't cook that night, it wasn't required. Both mother and daughter had afternoon's leftovers. At 11 pm Rajiv woke her up; she got scared to see him so furious. 'You don't even have the courtesy to keep some food for me. I am working so hard trying to impress my boss for the next promotion. Do you know what it takes to attend his parties and appreciate him for nothing? After all this, my wife quietly sleeps and doesn't even ask me if I want to eat.' Maya quietly got up, cooked a meal for him. She could never make a mistake of not keeping his clothes washed and ironed all the time as he hated even a bit wrinkled clothes.

Last month, on Maya's birthday, Sia gave her a greeting card. Maya knew that her daughter was really good in writing. She expected something very touchy and emotional from her. Sia wrote, 'Mummy, I love you a lot. I know I don't have much time for you these days. But I really love you and will never hide anything from you. You are the best Maa, and you know why because you cook really awesome food for me.' Maya was the happiest that day; it was after ages somebody called her cooking awesome.

She knew cooking since the age of seventeen. She had always loved to cook. And when it came to decorating her house, nobody could beat her. When they bought this flat, in a month's time she turned it into a beautiful haven of flowers and beautiful colours. She really had a taste in décor. She always wanted to be an interior decorator, but then she didn't want to be too busy making other's lives beautiful. She was happy to keep the skill restricted only to her own place. Rajiv used to get his friends home just to show off his wife's skills in décor.

But her interest in decorating and cooking had gone down drastically after years of marriage. She knew what the reason was. She knew that she expected some appreciation. She wanted some appreciation for her great cooking. She wanted somebody to hold her and tell her that she does a lot for her family. She was the one who held this family together. She was the one who took care of their hygiene, cleanliness and nutrition. She was the one who made this house, truly a home. So what, if she didn't go out and work; so what, if she didn't earn a penny and was financially dependent on her husband. So what? That didn't reduce her talent in any way. That didn't make her less in any way. She did not work because she wanted her family to be a priority, but is it really worth if the family didn't understand this. She wanted Rajiv to acknowledge just one small fact that she is important to him. She wanted to hear from him, just a few words of appreciation.

Coming back to the reality, she realized that she had to start working to be in time to prepare lunch and clean up the house to be guest-friendly.

She made a promise to herself to make it up for this missed opportunity. She told herself that she will go for a day out and will really enjoy. After all she also needed something to look forward. So what if Rajiv never appreciated her work – it doesn't mean that she wasn't good at what she was doing. She would take her life back in her own control in no time.

The Repentance

She was sitting with a wood-like expression on her face, not ready to accept what she just witnessed, not willing to give away the guilt of what she did. She was sitting outside the surgery room in Sankara eye hospital, waiting desperately, hoping that someone would give her relieving news.

Hoping that, someone would just come out and tell her that her husband Karan has not lost his vision. However being a medical doctor herself, she knew that she was hoping beyond hope. Karan's right eye could not have survived the damage. Damage, oh the damage, the blood, his painful cries, the panic, his anger, her screams, she was indeed living a nightmare.

It was not the pain of today or a few days, it was continuous stress that everybody had to pay for now. It was the stress of their marriage and their families. It was an arranged marriage; both the families knew each other since a couple of years before deciding on the alliance. Geeta and Karan accepted. A year into the marriage and they had regular fights because Karan's mom had a very sharp tongue and did not like Geeta's way of life. Geeta was tired of trying to keep up with the expectations of her mother-in-law. She had just not grown up that way, to do the household stuff; she hardly knew how to cook when she got married. She was a neurosurgeon after all, had spent half her life studying and was still struggling to complete her MD. Where did she have time to get up at 7 am to serve bed tea to her husband and her in-laws? She simply could not make both ends meet.

Karan felt too exhausted trying to make up between his mother and his wife. There was no way he could choose one over the other. There was no way he could blame the other person. It had been eight months since his mother moved in to live with them after his father was posted in Assam. After giving up on his mom and wife, he started staying out of the house most of the time. He would come back late from office, leave early morning, would work on weekends. Their sex life was totally non-existent. His mom would not understand how much she was damaging his life. She was too concerned about the fact that she wanted the kind of daughter-in-law that she was to her in-laws; she did not want another member in the family who needed to be taken care of because she is too busy with her career. The thought was too unacceptable to her. For her, daughters-in law were supposed to take care of the house, family and parents, even if she had to work outside, she still should be able to balance both in a way that former was not compromised. No matter how much Karan wanted her to understand that Geeta only had 24 hours in a day and she could only do so much with the given time and energy, she would not accept and would blame him for the taking his wife's side when his mother was getting old.

Today all hell broke loose, when Karan's mother blamed Geeta for not preparing porridge in the morning. It was a small thing, she should have just ignored the blame, but with so much negative inside her, she could not. After a petty argument with mother-in-law, Geeta went in to blame Karan for putting her through all this. She was after all his mother; he was supposed to make her understand. How much could Karan take in, in anger he just punched his fist into the wall. When that pain was not enough he went to hit his head on the wall. Geeta panicked and in the nick of the moment she tried to stop him from hitting his head. She couldn't. There was a nail on the wall and in all the confusion Karan's face hit on the wall with the nail exactly at the place of his eye socket. He screamed in pain, covering his right eye with his hand, there was blood oozing out of his fingers. She ran for some water, washed his face and his eyes with clean water. He could not open his eye at all and bleeding would not stop. He was rushed to the hospital; doctor suggested an immediate surgery to save the retina from the damage. There were no second thoughts; he was taken to the operation theatre.

Now, it was just Geeta and her mother-in-law waiting in the lobby for some news, hoping it was good. Both the ladies felt pathetic, guilty and almost dead. It was the man that both of them loved the most. Was all this really worth it? These fights, arguments, blame-games definitely are not worth Karan's vision. Did they even deserve to be forgiven? With blood stains on their clothes and tears in their eyes, they both looked at each other; they both knew what the other one was going through, yet their egos did not melt.

After some time, Geeta felt a warm hand on her shoulder, when she turned it was Karan's mother. The same face, same eyes, same hairstyle, yet there was something that was different. The expression, the softness, the sadness, which was something Geeta had never seen.

'It was an accident. I know you love him too much to make him do something silly like this,' mother said.

Geeta's vision became blurred because her eyes were full of tears now. 'Sorry maa. I am really sorry,' Geeta said and continued to cry on the mother's shoulder. After some time when she got tired of crying, she realized that there was a loving hand on her head and that she could smell the warmth of a mother. For some reason, she felt secure and taken care of. She felt that she was not alone to fight all this. She felt that somebody was there for her. And that somebody was the lady who had given birth to her husband. She was the lady because of whom Karan existed and was a part of her life. She was the lady who once fed Karan, who spent sleepless nights when he was sick.

That was the moment, which transformed the relationship of the mother- and daughter-in-law.

Why is it that we always wait for accidents to happen?

Why do wait for a person to be on a death bed to express our love for him/her?

Why do we always miss the person when the person ceases to exist?

Why do we always wait for the last moment to do the right thing?

Why do we keep running after things that aren't that important?

Why only when a tragedy happens, we realize our mistakes?

UNBORN SMILE

She had dreams for her – mighty, majestic dreams. She had waited for this feeling of motherhood since so long. Just a few days more and then they would be a family – her own family. She was longing to look at her daughter, her cute little hands and feet, her baby smile, innocent eyes and baby giggles.

'My daughter will have the best education in the world,' she said aloud. Nevertheless, her husband; Gaurav would always want her to be a MBBS-MD doctor. 'What if she liked to be a model or an actress? No, that world is way too glamorous and dangerous. How about a dancer or a singer?' She smiled at her imagination going so far, while caressing her huge belly. 'She'll have my eyes, pure black with long curly eye lashes. And there would be the perfect shape of nose just like her father's. She'll have long thick black hair flowing down her shoulders and a flawless fair complexion. Wow, she is going to grow up so beautiful!'

Shipra was surprised to see such a sudden transformation in Gaurav. Theirs was a love-cum-arranged marriage. They liked each other since childhood but their parents had decided them for each other. They were perfectly made for each other. After two years of lovely marriage, she knew him to be a serious, no nonsense types. He was usually busy with work, and she had to be really stubborn to have some parties and fun in life. However, the day he heard the news of his becoming a father, he tuned to an absolutely crazy school boy. He would come home laden with toys, dolls, balloons etc. He would dance with her for no reason at all. Though, she was advised not to eat outside food, he would still take her out for some healthy snacks.

Shipra was deep in her thoughts when the doorbell rang. Gaurav had returned. He made all the dinner and fed her with his own hands. She loved him even more but in a different way now, as she looked upon him as more of her child's father – a responsible man, not just a husband.

It was 2:30 in the morning. Although she was lying on the bed, the sleep was far from her. He was fast asleep tired after the day's hectic schedule. She was feeling really anxious but didn't want to disturb or worry him.

She closed her eyes thinking that it was the last minute anxiety and probably there was nothing to worry about. And in some time she was in darkness, sleeping peacefully. Suddenly she saw something far away, something bad and filthy. She couldn't understand but could only see something that made her even more anxious. And then she got aware of all the blood around her. She walked forward only to find dead bodies on the way, brutally murdered corpses. Her heart beat rose and she was scared to death. Her body was shaking from head to toe, sweating profusely. She heard some noises and turned to see a set of people running towards her with all kind of weapons and their clothes smothered in blood. She ran for her life and entered a very dark room at the corner of the street. There she saw a hazy figure of a child. The child moved forward and she saw those pure black eyes with curly lashes, perfect cut of the nose, long black hair and the flawless skin. Those innocent black eyes looked miserably into hers as if looking for an answer. Her lips muttered – 'Mamma, is this the kind of world you want me to come into? I wanted to be an actress but this is where I have landed where people won't even let me live.'

Before Shipra could say anything at all, she felt severe pain in her stomach and she found herself lying on the bed, next to Gaurav.

She cried as her husband panicked and rushed her to the hospital. She was screaming and shouting while people around her were preparing for her delivery. She saw Gaurav, his anxious eyes but still felt relieved. He was holding her hand, comforting her, asking her to relax. In few more hours in the delivery room, she felt a deadly pain and then everything went blank. After some time, which seem to her like a few hours, she opened her eyes and felt something missing. She got curious, anxious and very restless, and then somebody placed a beautiful infant in her lap. She was speechless and dumb-struck. She felt somebody's caring hand on her shoulder. When she looked up, he had tears in his eyes.

He sat by her side, congratulating her and for the first time in her life, she felt complete.

SEX STILL A TABOO

'O my God, I felt such shiver when he held my hand. I felt goose bumps all over my body. It was like magic when he kissed me on my cheeks. I could feel his breath so close,' thoughts were running high in Anita's mind. She had just came back home after meeting her boyfriend at school. Her boyfriend Abhishek had shown interest in her a week back. They both were sixteen years old. Their hormones were making them crazy right now. They had no idea what is happening to their bodies and their thought process. Today, Abhishek was so scared to just hold her hands and kiss her on cheeks. His friends were telling him that if she smiles and blushes, he should just go for her lips. However, he was worried that she might not like it. They did speak to each other on this. He asked her if she wanted to go ahead. She blushed and just nodded her head.

Anita just came back home and called her friend Jaya to tell her what happened. Jaya reacted very differently. She had expected Jaya to share her happiness but Jaya said, 'Are you crazy? Okay, you have done this much. Don't go ahead now. Tell him that he has to keep a distance from physically. You know guys are like this. He will try to kiss you on your lips and will want to touch your breasts and then have sex with you. How do you know if you won't get pregnant?'

Anita was very scared when she heard Jaya say all this. 'I trust him, Jaya. I know that he really loves me and will not use me just for sex. Please don't misunderstand him.' Said Anita defensively.

One month later, Anita was crying in her bed. She had dark circles under her eyes; she had not slept for two nights properly. She refused to meet any of her friends or talk to her parents about what happened. Her parents were worried and tried calling all her friends to find out what had happened to her, nobody knew a thing.

Abhishek was concerned with Anita's changed attitude. He tried to get in touch with her, but she wouldn't reply. He thought 'Why is she making such a big deal out of this? I thought I was making her happy, but she never seems easy to understand.' He knew that he shouldn't have tried to convince her that sex was a normal thing to do and people do it on a daily basis. He did not realize how much he wanted to touch her till they actually had a long kiss. His mind just got stuck. He wanted to touch her breasts and then her legs and then between the legs.

'I was just not able to think. It seemed like I knew the right thing to do. I cannot imagine that I really kissed a girl and touched her at places she has never been touched before. Her expressions were so different. I don't know if she really liked it. But I have never been so hard before. She did not stop me. If she did not like it, she could have stopped me anytime. I don't know what came over me that I tried to push inside her. I only knew it from the porn movies that I had seen. That's exactly what they do. But I think Anita was in pain and she asked me to stop. It took me some time to understand what she is saying. I think she is very upset with me. I hope she doesn't find out that I told all that happened to Rohit, Aadi and Ashu. She will be mad at me. I love her a lot but I had to tell my friends that I was the first one to have sex with a girl, now they can never make fun of me again. I am sure she will understand.'

'How could he do this? Jaya was right. It was all about sex. I loved it when he was touching me all over. But he just kept going. I was bleeding for god's sake. And he could not stop. I don't know what had gotten into him. I loved him, but I hate him now. I gave him everything I had, even my body and my soul. He almost became an animal just did not realize that it was painful for me. I am so upset. I don't know if I could be pregnant. Jaya told me that there is some sort of the liquid that comes out of the guy that can make the girl pregnant. I did not see any such liquid coming out of him. I don't know what that means. I don't know who I should talk to about this. Mom and Dad will kill me if they find out. Jaya will also be very angry. I cannot tell my sisters also; I don't know what they will think of me. What have I done to myself? I should have never met him. He used me.'

This small story of Anita and Abhishek is very common. These teenagers filled up with excitement because of their hormones going crazy in them. They have no idea what is happening to them. There are huge emotional and physical implications of what happened to Anita and Abhishek. They only depend on their friends and porn to know about sex and some silly magazines to understand what really happens.

What would have been so wrong if Anita had the freedom to talk to her parents when she initially felt his strong touch and so attracted to him?

Why was it that Anita had nobody to talk to right now?

Why was she feeling so ashamed of what she did?

Why was Abhishek not so considerate about what he did? Why did he think that his friends will consider him a 'James Bond' if he was first one to have sex?

Why did he not care anymore for her?

Why did he have to take inspiration from porn to have sex with Anita?

There is definitely something wrong in the way families are today, if this is the condition of teenagers today. Families are supposed to be the support system particularly for growing children. Instead of closing doors to sex and love, these should be openly discussed on dinner table.

Even today, an awkward situation arises when a commercial of condom or contraceptive pills or even sanitary napkins comes up when entire family is sitting and watching TV. Even more awkward situation comes up for parents when a seven-year old asks what a condom really is. We need to find a better way to tell a seven-year old about condoms without just changing the subject. Because when we scold a kid to not ask such questions or tell him/her that s/he is not supposed to know all this, we close the door to him/her when s/he grows up and comes into a situation like Abhishek or Anita.

We need to build a support system for our kids so that they know that they always have us behind them. They should know that they can take advice from us when they are confused and in doubt. Also, they should know that we will never stop loving them no matter what big blunder they do.